Dorothy and the Magic Belt

Dorothy and the Magic Belt

By Susan Saunders
Illustrated by David Rose

Random House 🏠 New York

For Dagmar, who introduced me to Oz.
—S.S.

Library of Congress Cataloging in Publication Data: Saunders, Susan. Dorothy and the magic belt. SUMMARY: Dorothy and her friends, the Tin Woodman, the Scarecrow, and Jack Pumpkinhead, travel across Oz in search of the young wizard who stole Princess Ozma's Magic Belt. 1. Children's stories, American. [1. Fantasy] I. Rose, David S., 1947– , ill. II. Title. PZ7.S2577Do 1985 [Fic] 84-17946 ISBN: 0-394-87067-0 (trade); 0-394-97067-5 (lib. bdg.)

Manufactured in the United States of America 1 2 3 4 5 6 7 8 9 0

Contents

An Unexpected Trip

It was a fine autumn day on the Kansas farm where Dorothy Gale lived. The fall harvest was in, corn filled the silo, and the wheat was on its way to market.

Most important, it was Saturday morning. And on Saturday mornings Princess Ozma, ruler of all the Land of Oz, looked at Dorothy in her magic picture. Or at least that's what Dorothy was telling her aunt Em and uncle Henry at breakfast.

"That's right," Dorothy said. "The picture

7

keeps changing, and it can show Ozma anyone or anyplace in the world she wants to see."

"Is that so?" said Uncle Henry.

"I declare!" said Aunt Em. She and Uncle Henry didn't know quite what to make of Dorothy's stories about the mysterious Land of Oz. Emerald cities, and talking animals, and their own little niece a princess with a crown . . . Aunt Em shook her head and sighed.

"It's true," Dorothy went on with a nod. "Every Saturday morning Princess Ozma in Oz looks at me, right here in Kansas. And if I make a certain signal, like this—"

But Aunt Em and Uncle Henry never got to hear the end of the sentence. Princess Ozma had indeed been looking at Dorothy in her magic picture. She and Dorothy had agreed that if she ever saw Dorothy's secret signal, Ozma would wish the girl to Oz as quick as a wink. And that's just what happened.

Aunt Em and Uncle Henry looked at Dorothy's half-eaten bowl of oatmeal and then at each other. Toto barked loudly at the empty chair. Dorothy had disappeared!

And by the time Dorothy had finished the sentence she had started back in Kansas, she was standing in the throne room in the Emerald Palace!

"Dorothy!" Golden-haired Princess Ozma gave the girl a welcoming hug. "We were beginning to wonder if you were *ever* coming to visit us!"

And Ozma wasn't the only one on hand to greet Dorothy. The Cowardly Lion purred with pleasure when he saw her.

The Hungry Tiger licked his lips and paid her his greatest compliment. "You're looking as delicious as ever," he told her.

The Yellow Hen, Billina, laid an egg right under the throne in Dorothy's honor. "If you like, you may have it for lunch," she offered generously. "It's absolutely fresh."

Highly Magnified Woggle-Bug, T.E. (which stands for Thoroughly Educated, of course), made a complicated speech crowded with very long words, entitled "My Feelings on Dorothy's Return to Oz." (As usual, everyone stopped listening after the opening sentences.)

And the Tik-Tok Man had himself wound up

extra-tight. "So I can talk to you for twen-ty-four hours with-out run-ning down," he informed Dorothy.

Dorothy was very happy and excited to see her old friends. But as she quickly explained, "It's

wonderful to be here again, but I'm afraid there's been a mistake! I was just telling Aunt Em and Uncle Henry about the magic picture—I never meant to leave them like that. I'll have to go right back," she finished sadly.

"Nonsense!" Billina squawked. "I have one hundred fourteen new chicks, all hatched since you were here last. You can't leave without at least seeing *them*."

"Aunt Em and Uncle Henry are going to be awfully worried about me," Dorothy said.

"We can take care of that," said Ozma. "Why don't you write them a note telling them where you are and how long you plan to stay. I'll use the magic belt to wish the note to them in Kansas."

"An ex-cell-ent idea," said the Tik-Tok Man.

"Indubitably," said the Woggle-Bug, not wanting to be outdone in the use of big words.

"I'd love to," Dorothy said slowly, thinking about it. "But they'll be so upset if I get behind in school."

"Get behind in school!" H. M. Woggle-Bug spoke up indignantly, his antennae quivering. "Am I not the official public educator of Oz and president of the college? A few classes with me, and you will be so far ahead you may never have to go to school again."

"Well . . ." Dorothy said. "Maybe it would be all right if I stayed for a little while."

12

Ozma clapped her hands with delight—it would be such fun having Dorothy in the palace again, even for a little while. She called to Jellia Jamb, her lady-in-waiting, to bring pen and paper.

Then Dorothy sat down to write a note to her aunt and uncle. "Dear Aunt Em and Uncle Henry," she began. "Please don't worry. I am in Oz with the princess and my other friends . . ."

"Why don't you tell them that we will watch them in the magic picture?" Ozma suggested. "If they agree that you may stay for a few days, they can wave to us."

Dorothy quickly finished her letter, signed it, and handed it to Ozma. Ozma held the piece of paper in one hand and touched her magic belt with the other. Then the letter was gone, on its way to Kansas.

Ozma and Dorothy and the others turned to the magic picture. First it changed so quickly that the lands flashing through it were almost a blur. Then Dorothy saw mountains and hills and lakes, and finally the flat plains that run straight down the middle of the United States.

There was the old farmhouse, like a faded gray

box dropped in a field of brown autumn stubble. Toto was snoozing in the sunshine on the front porch.

Now they could see inside the house . . . Aunt Em and Uncle Henry were reading the letter . . . they were talking to each other about it . . . they stared nervously around, perhaps wondering exactly which direction to face. Finally they both waved, hesitantly at first, then as hard as they could.

"It's all right!" Dorothy said. "I can stay!"

"Jellia Jamb," Princess Ozma directed, "have the cooks prepare a magnificent banquet. Tonight we will celebrate the return of our own Dorothy."

A Family Business

At about the same time that Dorothy was sitting down at her breakfast table in Kansas, a young man was jumping up from his breakfast table in the Gillikin Country of Oz.

"Turnips for breakfast?" he shouted. He stamped the floor of the cave with his sturdy purple boot. (Because he was a Gillikin, the young man's clothes were all purple. And he and his old father lived in a cave—a clean, spacious cave, to be sure, but still a cave.)

"Don't excite yourself, Nik," said his father, tugging worriedly at his long white beard. "It's turnips because I seem to grow turnips best."

"That's because you're not a farmer!" his son said. "You're a wizard! So why don't you act like one? Conjure up a good breakfast!"

"Son, you know as well as I do that the good witch Glinda has forbidden the practice of magic in Oz," his father said for the umpteenth time. "Except for herself and the Princess Ozma in the Emerald City, of course," he added.

"Glinda and the princess! Glinda and the princess!" the young man stormed. "Just because they say so, you give up a perfectly good business handed down from father to son for hundreds of years?" He kicked a leg of the table, and a purple turnip rolled off his plate.

"One doesn't argue with Glinda," his father said firmly.

"Maybe *you* don't!" said the young man. And with that he slammed out of the cave, leaving his father to shake his head sadly.

Nikidik the Younger—he was called that because his father's name was Nikidik too—took

16

the path that led up the side of the mountain above the cave. When he reached the top, he looked to the south, toward the Emerald City.

"My father was one of the most famous wizards of all Gillikin Country," he muttered. "And that's what *I* should be. I'm not going to waste my life growing turnips and living in a cave."

Nik knew that Glinda was no one to trifle with—she had the most powerful magic in Oz. But he also knew about Princess Ozma's magic belt. Practically everyone had heard about the wonderful belt. It had once belonged to the evil Nome King. And it was said that it not only had the power to transport people anywhere at all, but it could also transform anything into anything else.

"If I had that belt," Nikidik the Younger said to himself, "the first thing I would transform would be our cave . . . into a beautiful purple palace."

Wasn't Nik afraid of being punished by the good witch Glinda?

"The belt would protect me," Nik said. "And if that didn't work, I could wish myself somewhere else and she'd have a very hard time catching me."

He had made up his mind. He would leave immediately for the Emerald City. By tomorrow, with luck, he, Nikidik the Younger, would have the magic belt.

But how? How could a young man with no magic powers walk into the Emerald Palace, past the guard at the gates and the soldier at the door, not to mention the Cowardly Lion—who was really not a coward—and the Hungry Tiger— who was always looking for a tasty treat—and take the princess's most valued possession?

Ah, but Nik had a few things up his sleeve. And on top of the mountain in Gillikin Country, he reached up that sleeve and pulled them out. First a book of ancient magic spells, written by his great-great-great-great-great-grandfather Nikidik centuries before.

"This is all there is left," he murmured, stroking the book. "This and the powders. If I hadn't saved them from the bonfire, my father would have destroyed them along with everything else . . . just because Glinda said so!"

Next Nik pulled out a small purple jar. DR. NIKIDIK'S AGING POWDER, the label read. Last he removed a large packet tied with purple string. "And Youthing Powder," Nik said. He thought long and hard, then replaced all three items in his wide sleeve.

"I think it will work," he said. "The Nikidik family will soon be back in business—the business of magic."

And Nikidik the Younger started purposefully down the mountain, heading south toward the Emerald City.

The Purple Cloud

Dorothy woke up early the next morning in her bedroom in the Emerald Palace. The sun was just brightening the pale green curtains—it was going to be a beautiful day in the Land of Oz.

Dorothy didn't want to stay in bed a minute longer. But the palace was quiet, so she knew her friends—Princess Ozma, the Cowardly Lion, the Hungry Tiger, and H.M. Woggle-Bug—were still sleeping. The banquet in her honor had gone on quite late the night before.

Then she remembered the Sawhorse, who hadn't been at the banquet. Besides, the creature was made of wood and never slept. If the Sawhorse was in a good mood, perhaps it would take her for a ride before breakfast.

The Sawhorse had been with Ozma since before she was Ozma, when she was still the boy Tip, under a spell put on her by Old Mombi, a witch. Now it had a beautiful stall in the royal stables.

Dorothy hopped out of bed. She chose something to wear from a closet stuffed with clothes made just for her by the royal seamstresses. Then she slipped soundlessly out of the palace to look for the Sawhorse.

Although the Sawhorse's ears were handmade, they were very sharp ones. When it heard the girl enter the stables, it poked its wooden head around the stall door.

"Dorothy!" the creature greeted her. "Back in Oz so soon?" Which could have sounded rude, but it was really only the Sawhorse's gruff way of talking, because the next thing it said was, "How about an early-morning gallop across the fields?"

And that was exactly what Dorothy wanted.

The Soldier with the Green Whiskers was not yet at his post at the door to the palace. And the Guardian of the Gates was dozing in a chair as they approached the gates in the wall around the Emerald City. He woke with a start at the sound of the Sawhorse's gold-shod hoofs tapping on the paving stones. The guardian gave horse and rider a sleepy salute. Then his head fell forward on his chest—he was sleeping again.

For all its peculiar appearance, the Sawhorse was as swift as the wind. And because both legs on one side of the creature moved forward together, then both legs on the other side, riding the Sawhorse was as pleasant as being in a rocking chair. It carried Dorothy miles to the east of the Emerald City in minutes.

The grass under its feet shaded from emerald green to blue, and soon they were racing through Munchkin Country. They passed quaint blue farmhouses, and milkmaids in blue aprons holding buckets of light-blue milk, and shepherds in blue cloaks herding blue-spotted sheep.

If Dorothy and the Sawhorse had gone north,

they might have noticed a serious-looking young man, dressed in the purple clothes of the Gillikins, approaching the green granite walls of the Emerald City. This was Nikidik the Younger, nearing the end of his journey, which had begun the morning before.

A little way from the gates, Nik reached up his wide sleeve and pulled out the two magic powders he had hidden there. The Aging Powder could make everyone in the Emerald Palace grow very old very fast. And the Youthing Powder could do just the opposite, which seemed nicer somehow. Weren't people always saying they wished they were younger?

Nikidik wasn't a terrible young man. He didn't want to hurt the inhabitants of the palace. On the other hand, he didn't want to get hurt himself when he tried to take Ozma's magic belt.

"If I make those living in the palace very much younger," he reasoned, "they won't even know what the magic belt is, much less how to use it against me. Then I can walk right into the palace and take it for my own."

Nikidik replaced the jar of Aging Powder in his

sleeve. He carefully opened the packet of Youthing Powder and poured a little bit onto the palm of his left hand. He closed his fingers around it and stuck the packet into his pocket. He was ready.

The Guardian of the Gates was wide awake now, and he gave Nikidik a friendly greeting as he approached: "Good morning, young sir. You're our first visitor this fine day."

Nik raised his left hand and let a bit of the lavender powder drift down in front of the plump guard's nose.

"What . . . ?" the guardian exclaimed, but he breathed, he sneezed . . . and suddenly he was a youth of about fifteen, the green uniform hanging on his now-slender frame.

He looked around, then at Nikidik. "Why am I out here, dressed like this?" he said. "My mother will be angry if I'm late to breakfast!" With that, he rushed away, leaving the gates unguarded.

Nik smiled. This was going to be easy.

The next person he met was the Soldier with the Green Whiskers, who stood in front of the enormous door to the palace. He had a curly green beard that reached almost to his knees and shimmered in the sun. But after he had been given a dose of Nik's Youthing Powder, not only was his beard gone, but his mustache too.

The soldier put down his sword and wandered

away from his post. He scratched his head in a puzzled way, as though he were trying to remember something important.

Nik pulled out the packet of powder again. He hadn't forgotten Ozma's fierce friends, the gigantic lion and tiger, who had rooms in the palace. And he was taking no chances. He poured at least a cupful of powder into his hand. Then he blew it into the air. It rose and rose, higher and higher, and spread out into a pale purple cloud that hovered over the palace.

Nik was careful not to breathe any of the cloud himself. He held a handkerchief over his nose and mouth until the cloud had faded and disappeared. Then, cautiously, he entered the palace.

Nik hurried across the glittering throne room and down the hall on the other side that led to the bedrooms. The Cowardly Lion and the Hungry Tiger had slept with their windows wide open. They had breathed enough of the cloud of Youthing Powder to become the half-grown kittens they once were. They were so busy batting a ball around on the green marble floor that they hardly looked up as Nikidik rushed past.

And the Woggle-Bug was no longer Highly Magnified. He had returned to the size he had been as a young bug, about the size of a pea. He was much too small for Nik to even notice, though the insect scurried down the hall right in front of him.

The windows in Ozma's bedroom had been halfway open. And she had turned back into Tip, the young boy she had been under Mombi's spell in the earlier part of her life. Tip knew nothing about the magic belt, or even where he was, so he didn't object when Nikidik walked into Ozma's bedroom. All Tip wanted to know was why he, a boy, was dressed in a nightgown.

Nikidik caught his breath at the sight of the magic belt. It lay on Ozma's dresser, its hundreds of jewels catching the light and turning it into tiny rainbows. And it was his for the taking.

He picked it up and buckled it around his waist. Leaving Tip to dig through Ozma's closet, trying to find a sensible pair of trousers, Nik stepped back out into the hall. He was ready to go home and find out exactly what his treasure could do.

"And there is no need for Nikidik to walk," he said gleefully, "ever again." He put his hand on the magic belt and wished himself back to the top of the mountain in Gillikin Country.

Nik had not seen Tik-Tok, the copper man, standing in the shadows. But Tik-Tok had seen him. And heard him too.

4

Dorothy Goes for Help

The Sawhorse and its rider, Dorothy, had turned back toward the Emerald City after a very exciting run. Suddenly the girl thought she saw a pale purple cloud hanging over the palace. She rubbed her eyes and looked again. But the cloud was no longer there.

"It must have been a reflection of some sort," Dorothy decided.

And the Sawhorse agreed: "The sun sometimes plays tricks."

31

As soon as they arrived at the gates to the city, however, they felt that something was wrong. The Guardian of the Gates was nowhere in sight, which was very strange. And as they passed through the gates into the city itself, they noticed many small children crawling around and crying and trotting aimlessly back and forth—many more than there would usually be, with no adults taking care of them. (Just minutes before, all of those children *had* been adults. Unknowingly they had breathed the Youthing Powder in the purple cloud.)

Then Dorothy and the Sawhorse spotted the

Soldier with the Green Whiskers. At least they thought it was he. He was wearing the right uniform, and there was only one soldier in the Emerald City. But he no longer had any whiskers at all. He was spinning a top. And he didn't seem to recognize them.

"There's something funny going on here," said the Sawhorse. But he didn't sound amused.

"Let's hurry to the palace," Dorothy said. "I'm sure Ozma can tell us what this is all about."

But what they found at the palace was much more distressing. Billina was in the courtyard, or at least a fluffy yellow chick who *used* to be Billina

was there. Around the chick's neck was a necklace that Billina never took off, so Dorothy and the Sawhorse knew it was their old friend.

The Cowardly Lion and the Hungry Tiger were large playful kittens. And Princess Ozma was gone. In her place was a young boy named Tip.

The Sawhorse knew Tip, of course. "This is Ozma as she was in the old days," it explained to Dorothy. "Time appears to be running backward."

And the Tik-Tok Man seemed to bear this out. He was made of metal, so the Youthing Powder hadn't made him younger. But it had jammed up his works very thoroughly.

When Dorothy wound him up to see if he could tell her anything, he ran backward. He crashed into the wall behind him as he repeated a word: "Kidikin, kidikin, kidikin." Which was a very good clue, but it meant nothing to Dorothy or the Sawhorse.

"Maybe the magic belt can stop this awful enchantment!" Dorothy said.

But the magic belt was nowhere to be found. In fact, it was already in Gillikin Country.

"Perhaps we will just have to wait until they all grow up again," said the Sawhorse gloomily.

"What if they get younger and younger, until they disappear altogether?" Dorothy asked. "No—we have to get help, and quick!"

The good witch Glinda was too far away. Her palace was all the way south on the other side of Quadling Country, at the edge of the Great Sandy Waste. But what about the Tin Woodman and the Scarecrow? They shared the Woodman's castle in Winkie Country.

"Jack Pumpkinhead is there too," the Sawhorse said, "for what that's worth."

Jack was a very nice fellow, but he wasn't known for his brains. But the Scarecrow was—he had the finest brains in the land, given to him by the Wizard of Oz himself.

"The Scarecrow will know what to do!" Dorothy said.

So for the second time that morning, Dorothy and the Sawhorse sped away from the Emerald City. They were off to the Tin Woodman's castle just as fast as the Sawhorse's golden feet could fly.

Tik-Tok's Clue

A Winkie in a handsome blue uniform covered with gold braid led Dorothy and the Sawhorse up the steps and into the castle of his majesty, Nick Chopper, emperor of Winkie Country. This was the Tin Woodman, of course, and he was overjoyed to see his old friend Dorothy. He couldn't move for the moment, because he was being polished all over with very fine steel wool by four Winkie tinsmiths. But he blew Dorothy a kiss.

"What a surprise!" he said. "We were just preparing to go to the Emerald City to see you! Ozma had sent us word," he added.

"Something terrible has happened!" Dorothy cried. "Where is the Scarecrow?"

"In the next room, but—" the Tin Woodman began.

Dorothy had already opened the door and looked in. "What's wrong with him?" she gasped.

The Scarecrow was lying flat on the floor . . . very flat indeed. In fact, he wasn't much thicker than a sheet of paper.

"I'm fine," he reassured Dorothy, "newly washed, dried, and *pressed,*" which explained his extremely flat condition. "I'm just waiting to be stuffed with clean, fresh straw." He raised his flat

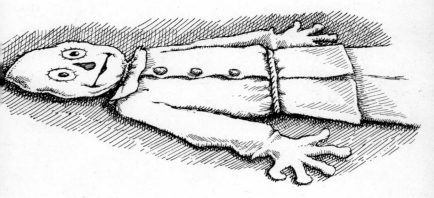

head a little. "It's certainly good to see you, my dear," he said, "but what terrible thing has happened?"

So she told the Tin Woodman and the Scarecrow the whole strange story, and the Sawhorse added a word or two here and there. Dorothy ended with the peculiar behavior of Tik-Tok.

And it was that part of the story the Scarecrow found most interesting. "He said, 'Kidikin, kidikin,'" repeated the Scarecrow. "And he was definitely running backward?"

"Definitely," said Dorothy.

"So you turn the word around, or forward," the Scarecrow said thoughtfully, "and you get . . . Nikidik!"

"Nikidik!" echoed Nick Chopper. "Why, that was the old Gillikin wizard who used to trade magical secrets with Mombi the witch." Then he shook his head. "I'm sure he has given up the business of magic."

"Still," said the Scarecrow, "it's a place to start. Where does Nikidik live?"

For the answer to that, they sent for Jack

Pumpkinhead. Jack had been raised a Gillikin himself, or at least a Gillikin's pumpkin.

His head had been feeling a little cold and damp, so he was down in the kitchen, standing close to the stove. When he walked into the room, he smelled a lot like a warm pumpkin pie.

As the Sawhorse had implied earlier, the Pumpkinhead was not very smart. So Jack was especially pleased when he could answer the question the Scarecrow asked him about Nikidik.

"It was one of Nikidik's magic powders that gave me life, you know," Jack said proudly. "He lives in a cave in the Gillikin Mountains, not far from Mombi's house."

The friends looked at a map of Oz. The distance from the Tin Woodman's castle to the Gillikin Mountains was about the same as to the Emerald City.

"It's not so far," Dorothy said.

"Nor will it take us through a dangerous part of Oz," noted the Scarecrow. (Although Ozma ruled all of Oz, there were still some strange people and places in the land.)

"If Nikidik does have the magic belt," the Tin

Woodman said grimly, "the danger will be at the end, when we find him."

"Why can't Glinda help us?" Jack asked. He was very wary of Nikidik's magic.

"It would take much too long for us to reach her," answered the Scarecrow.

"But it wouldn't take the Sawhorse so long," Jack pointed out sensibly.

So the friends decided to split up. Dorothy, the Tin Woodman, the Scarecrow, and Jack Pumpkinhead would go ahead with their search for Nikidik. The Sawhorse would speed across Oz to the palace of Glinda the Good.

The wooden horse left immediately. And as soon as the Scarecrow was restuffed with fresh straw, and the Tin Woodman had sharpened his axe, and Jack had dried his head thoroughly, and Dorothy had eaten something—since she was the only real person—the four of them set out on the trail of Nikidik.

They walked all day, into the evening, and all through the night. The Scarecrow, who was the softest and most comfortable, carried Dorothy while she slept. Early the next morning the four

companions stood at the foot of the Gillikin Mountains . . . and stared in amazement. At the top of the nearest peak was a grand palace, with turrets and towers of dark purple crystal.

"I never noticed that beautiful castle before," said Jack Pumpkinhead.

"I'm sure that's because it was never there before," the Scarecrow said kindly.

"Mysterious palaces popping up in unexpected places," said the Tin Woodman. "The magic belt can't be far away now." He swung his axe a few times. "Shall we proceed?"

6

Nikidik's Second Big Mistake

Nikidik the Younger had been a wizard for only twenty-four hours, and already he was in trouble. His first big mistake, of course, had been putting a spell on Princess Ozma and her friends and stealing the magic belt. His second big mistake had to do with Old Mombi, the witch.

As soon as Nik wished himself back to his mountaintop, he laid his purple handkerchief neatly on the ground. Touching the magic belt around his waist, he said, "Turn this purple handkerchief into a palace of purple crystal, as grand as the Emerald Palace, with lots of court-yards and fountains and furniture jeweled with amethysts." And in seconds there it was. It even had bright purple flags flying from the towers, snapping in the breeze.

"Perfect," Nik said. "Now I'm going to move Dad out of the cave and up here with me."

But the older Nikidik wanted to have nothing to do with it. In fact, he was horror-struck. "I don't know how you've done this," he said. "And I don't want to know. But Glinda will find out about it soon enough. I want to be as far away from here as I can get when she does."

"But Dad," said Nikidik the Younger, "I've got the magic belt. We have nothing to fear from Glinda."

"Speak for yourself," said his father, hurriedly stuffing several turnips into an overnight bag. "I have a feeling that when I see you again, you'll be older and wiser." And with that Nikidik the Older rushed out of his cave and down the mountain, disappearing into the woods.

So Nik the Younger climbed back up the mountain and wished himself one hundred new suits of clothes. He spent several hours trying them on. But there was no one there to admire them. And Nik was getting lonely.

"Magic Belt," he said then, "I want thirty courtiers in my palace, right now." And there they were, thirty fine ladies and gentlemen, all beautifully dressed. But because they weren't real people with real lives, they weren't very interesting or very much fun. So Nik wished them away again.

Then Nikidik tried to perform a few of the spells in the ancient book written by his five-times-great-grandfather. But most of them failed. He did manage to turn a toad into a turnip, which was not worth repeating.

"What I need," he decided, "is a real person to talk to about magic, someone who will give me pointers. But who could that be?"

Then he thought of Mombi, which was the beginning of his second big mistake.

Mombi had been a witch, almost as good at potions and spells as Nik's father. It was true that Glinda had taken Old Mombi's knowledge of magic away from her some time before, for casting spells when she wasn't supposed to. But if Nik made the old witch young, she would remember everything again. He decided to try it.

Nik would use the magic belt to whisk Mombi to his purple palace. But first he unbuckled the belt. He rebuckled it inside his shirt, next to his skin. Then he pulled his shirt down over it. Nik had no special reason to mistrust Mombi . . . but for now, he would keep the belt a secret.

He pulled the Youthing Powder out of his pocket and poured a little into his hand. Then he wished Mombi to the palace.

Mombi arrived in a very bad mood, with a brown cow and a half-empty pail of milk.

"Just what is all this?" she demanded. "One minute I'm in the barn, milking my cow and minding my own business. The next minute, without so much as a by-your-leave, I'm zipped to who knows where." She glowered disagreeably. "Half the milk is spilled, and now the cow is so nervous that she probably won't give any more." Mombi looked Nik right in the eye and said nastily, "It's witchcraft, that's what it is. Wouldn't that meddling Glinda like to hear all about it?"

But Nik ignored her outburst. *I just hope she'll be more pleasant when she's younger,* he thought to himself. And he gave her a sprinkle of Youthing Powder, with another sprinkle for good measure.

The years fell away, and suddenly Mombi was an attractive young woman about Nik's age. "Where am I?" she asked. "And who are you?"

"I'm Nikidik," Nik said.

"Don't be silly," Mombi said sharply. "I *know* Nikidik. He's short and round, and he looks nothing like you."

"*That* Nikidik is my father," young Nik explained.

"I don't see how it's possible, since he's not much older than you are," Mombi said. "But more to the point, where am I, and what do you want?"

"This is my palace," Nik said, "and I thought we might get to be friends, trade magical secrets, that kind of thing."

"Hmmmm," said Mombi, "trade magical secrets." She gazed greedily around the great purple hall with its crystalline walls and jeweled furniture. She knew very well that the palace hadn't been built in the usual way, stone by stone. If this

48

young man, whoever he was, had a spell to conjure up a palace like this one, that would be a spell
worth knowing. But she tried to hide her interest.

"What spells do you have to trade that I don't
already know?" she asked shrewdly.

Nik thought quickly. He knew Mombi wouldn't
be interested in turning toads into turnips, and
nothing else he had tried had really worked out.
But he could see that she was impressed with his
palace. So he decided to bluff.

"What about spells for palaces?" he asked slyly.

"I think first we should each give a demonstra-
tion of some *little* thing we can do," Mombi said.

"A good idea," Nik agreed. After all, he had
the magic belt—he could do just about anything.
"Why don't you go first?" he said politely.

Mombi nodded. She pointed at her cow, who

was wandering around, mooing mournfully. "Crickety," Mombi said. "Crackety. Crau." Mombi bowed twice and pulled her ear. "Turn to stone what once was a cow."

Bingo! The cow was a brown marble statue standing in the middle of the great hall.

Nik was delighted—Mombi remembered her magic, and it still worked! "It looks very lifelike," he said of the cow. "May I try your spell?"

Mombi nodded.

So Nik pointed at a pink butterfly perched on a window sill. "Crickety. Crackety. Crau." He stopped and said to Mombi, "It's not going to rhyme."

"It doesn't matter," Mombi snapped. "This incantation always works."

Nik repeated the words. Then he bowed twice and pulled on his ear. "Turn to stone what was once . . . a butterfly." Zap! The butterfly was now made of rose quartz.

"Neat trick!" said Nik. He liked being a wizard.

"Your turn," said Mombi.

Nik didn't know the words for any magic spells. But he could make them up as he went along. He spotted a little mouse in the corner of the great hall, washing its face. "Rickety. Tickety. Flynn," said Nik. He spun around twice and pointed at the mouse. "The mouse is gold!"

And the mouse *was* gold. This time it was the magic belt at work, not Nik's fake spell. But Mombi didn't know about the belt.

And when she tried the spell herself on a ladybug, it seemed to work again—but only because Nik secretly wished the belt to turn the ladybug into gold.

Mombi seemed satisfied that the spell was genuine.

"So we'll trade magical secrets?" Nik asked.

And Mombi quickly agreed.

Then Nik said, "I've had a very long day. I would like to have dinner in my rooms and then go to bed."

Mombi said she would like the same. Nik led the young witch to an enormous bedroom at one end of the great hall, wished a delicious dinner on a tea tray for her, and left her until the next day.

"Let's start early tomorrow morning," Nik said. "There is so much I can learn from you." He was feeling a bit smug, because he would be getting a great deal—Mombi's magical knowledge—and giving nothing in return, because he had no magical knowledge.

"Tomorrow morning," Mombi said. But she had a naturally suspicious mind. She waited until the middle of the night, when she was sure Nik was asleep. Then she crept out into the great hall and waited for a mouse. Soon one came skittering across the floor, perhaps a relative of the first mouse.

"Rickety," said Mombi. "Tickety. Flynn." She spun around twice and pointed at the mouse. "The mouse is gold," she finished.

Of course, nothing happened. It wasn't a real spell. And Nik wasn't there with the magic belt to make it work.

Mombi didn't seem surprised, however. "A spell that starts out 'Rickety, tickety, flynn' doesn't even sound authentic," she muttered. "There is much more to this young man than meets the eye. And tomorrow morning I intend to find out exactly what it is."

Two Big Babies

Early the next morning, while Mombi and Nik were still asleep in the purple palace, Dorothy and her friends started to climb the path up the side of the Gillikin Mountains. They hadn't walked far when they came upon Nikidik's cave. The door was closed and double-locked, and there was a note tacked to it: NIKIDIK THE OLDER WILL BE GONE INDEFINITELY ... OR UNTIL NIKIDIK THE YOUNGER COMES TO HIS SENSES.

"Nikidik the Younger?" said Dorothy. "I didn't know there was one."

"I never heard of one either," the Scarecrow said.

"Younger than what?" asked Jack.

"We shall ask about it," said the Tin Woodman, "at the grand and glorious palace." He glared at the palace disapprovingly.

"It's not nearly as nice as the Emerald Palace," Dorothy added loyally.

"But almost?" said Jack. He thought it was very beautiful, especially the purple Gillikin color.

It was also very quiet. The Emerald Palace was always full of life, with lots of people—and creatures—coming and going. But this huge purple palace seemed deserted.

"Where is everybody?" Jack asked.

"We'll soon find out," said the Tin Woodman. He led them up the curved steps and into the great hall.

"Not much in the way of furnishings," commented the Scarecrow. "A life-size statue of a cow in brown marble standing right in the middle of things?"

Then Nikidik the Younger entered the hall and stared at the strange group of friends.

The Tin Woodman turned to face the young man. "Nikidik?" he said.

Nik nodded. "Nikidik the Younger," he answered.

"We've come for the magic belt," said the Tin Woodman. He shifted his axe meaningfully.

"What magic belt?" Nik asked innocently.

"The magic belt you stole from Princess Ozma," said Dorothy. "After you made time run backward."

"The Tik-Tok Man saw you do it!" the Scarecrow said accusingly.

Jack Pumpkinhead said nothing—he had spotted Mombi at the other side of the great hall. He was trying very hard to decide where he had seen her before. (Mombi looked much younger than she had when Jack knew her, which was confusing.)

But Mombi paid no attention to Jack or any of the others. Now she had the answer to the puzzle. Nikidik the Younger was no wizard. It was a magic belt that had turned the mouse into gold, and turned her ladybug into gold as well. Undoubtedly it was the magic belt that had produced this fabulous palace. So it was the magic belt that she, Mombi, must have for her own.

"Where is it?" the Tin Woodman was asking Nik.

And without thinking, Nik put his hands on the belt, buckled under his shirt.

"Aha!" Mombi said.

When he heard her speak, Jack knew who she was. "Mombi!" he shrieked. He dived out of her way so quickly that his pumpkin head rolled off his body and under a chair. *At least part of me is safe*, he thought.

The Scarecrow and the Tin Woodman each grabbed one of Dorothy's hands and pulled her behind a huge crystal table, out of the line of fire. Mombi was already muttering the words to a spell and pointing at Nikidik the Younger.

"Don't you know the belt protects me from the magic of others?" Nik scoffed. "You can't harm me."

"Oh no?" screeched Mombi. She pointed at the brown marble cow and made some magical signs.

The stone animal began to move forward, slowly at first, then faster and faster. It was lumbering straight toward Nik!

Nik stood his ground. "Stop that thing!" he commanded the magic belt. But perhaps the spell was too strong, or perhaps the belt didn't work against brown marble. The cow kept right on coming.

Nik started to run, but he tripped over the legs of Jack Pumpkinhead's body. As he went down he remembered the Youthing Powder still in his pocket.

Nik pulled the Youthing Powder out and blew all that was left at the great stone cow. Some of it drifted into the face of Mombi the witch. Unfortunately for Nik, in his hurry he breathed quite a lot of the powder himself.

Nik, the stone cow, and Mombi all began to change, growing younger . . . and younger.

"They're all babies!" Dorothy exclaimed.

And so they were. The stone cow was now a frisky calf, frolicking around the great hall. Mombi was still in a temper, red-faced and crying loudly. Nik wriggled away from the noise, crawling out of the magic belt, which was now much too big for him.

Dorothy ran around the table and grabbed the belt. And it was just at that moment that the Sawhorse burst into the great hall. On its back was Glinda the Good, seated on a saddle of white satin.

"My friends!" Glinda said when she saw Dorothy, the Tin Woodman, and the Scarecrow. "I see that you have found the magic belt, so all will be well." Then she looked hard at the babies.

"And here we have Nikidik the Younger—the very much younger—and . . . could it be Mombi?"

Glinda gave a silvery laugh. "Her disposition is no better as a baby than it was as an old woman."

Glinda climbed down from the Sawhorse and picked up Jack's fallen head. With the help of the Tin Woodman and the Scarecrow, she got his body to its feet and put the head back in place.

"Jack," she told the Pumpkinhead—Glinda always knew everything—"if you hadn't tripped Nikidik, things might have gone much, much worse."

And Jack bowed so low that his head almost fell off again.

"The magic belt will take care of things in the Emerald City, and we will wish ourselves there in a moment," Glinda continued. "But what shall we do here?"

"I see a jar of Aging Powder," the Scarecrow said. "Shall we sprinkle some on the babies?"

"We could," Glinda said thoughtfully. "On the other hand, perhaps we should speak with Nikidik the Older first. Dorothy, since you have the magic belt, would you please wish him here?"

In seconds old Nikidik was standing in the great purple hall, still carrying his bag of turnips. He paled when he saw Glinda. "I had nothing to do with this, Your Worship," he said. "Who are these babies? And where is my son?"

"You have nothing to fear," Glinda assured him. "And that baby is your son. The other is Mombi," she added.

"Please excuse the boy," old Nikidik said. "He really means no harm. But it's very hard when the work that your family has done for generations is taken away. He has been very unhappy." Nikidik the Older sighed and admitted, "So have I."

Glinda looked at him gravely. She picked up the book of ancient spells that Nik the Younger had saved and leafed through it. Toward the end of the book were some pages that she read carefully.

"You know that you are not allowed to practice real magic in Oz," she said to old Nikidik. "But I see here that your four-times-great-grandfather—besides being a wizard—made fabulous fireworks, which are themselves a kind of magic. There are so many parties and celebrations in Oz that fireworks would always be in demand." She added with a smile, "Much more so than turnips."

Nikidik beamed. "What a wonderful idea!" he said. "I'll try it."

"Shall we make your son older?" Glinda asked him.

"No . . . " said old Nikidik. "Since he's a baby again, I'll have a second chance at raising him properly. And Mombi, too," he added. "She'll be my dear adopted daughter."

"Good luck!" snorted the Sawhorse.

Old Nikidik gave Glinda the jar of Aging Powder, and all the pages of the ancient book that weren't about fireworks. Then he picked up the two babies and walked down the mountain. The little brown calf followed close behind.

Before old Nik had gotten to his cave, Dorothy, Glinda the Good, the Tin Woodman, the Scarecrow, the Sawhorse, and Jack Pumpkinhead were back in the Emerald City. And the purple palace was gone forever.

Home to Kansas

Back in the Emerald City, there was no need to sprinkle Aging Powder on everyone who had grown younger. Besides, there certainly would not have been enough to go around. The magic belt did it all, in a flash.

There was Princess Ozma, and Billina looking her old self, and the Woggle-Bug as Highly Magnified as ever, and the Cowardly Lion and the Hungry Tiger the right size, and Tik-Tok running forward as he was supposed to.

Tik-Tok was the hero of the day. Without his clue, who knows what might have happened? Ozma presented the copper man with an enormous platinum medal, diamond-encrusted, in appreciation.

Dorothy had a few peaceful days of visiting with all her friends, and then it was time to go home.

"Just think," said Jack Pumpkinhead, "if we hadn't found the magic belt, Dorothy might have been stranded in Oz for a very long time."

"I could think of worse things," said Dorothy.

Then, after some hugs and some waves and some tears, she was on her way back to Kansas. Until next time.